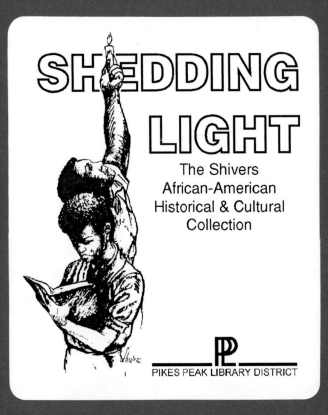

SHEDDING LIGHT

The Shivers
African-American
Historical & Cultural
Collection

PIKES PEAK LIBRARY DISTRICT

Freedom's a-Callin Me

Poems by Ntozake Shange

Paintings by Rod Brown

Amistad
An Imprint of HarperCollinsPublishers

Collins
An Imprint of HarperCollinsPublishers

FREEDOM'S A-CALLIN ME

the overseer's got his hands busy

ah hear that whip bouncin off somebody's back

bouncin like thousands of toddlers yelpin

but it aint but one or two slave aint pickin quick 'nough

but he aint lookin over here

this here is my chance to get

right out of here

mix my self way low in the cotton / most close to the dirt

wind myself like a snake

till ah can swim 'cross the stream

then them dogs'll lose my scent

it's like that over & over

in cold / in the winter / in the marsh / in a abandoned shanty

ah might get hungry

ah may get tired

good Lawd /

ah may may be free

NEVER AGAIN

he got us hangin like hogs or fresh beef beatin us

with us wigglin under /

under a rawhide whip

like that goin to scare us

we done taste some spittle from all his screamin

"never again" fall on deaf ears

ah feel my blood slidin down my back

welts risin up my arms

but we'll try try again

freedom aint a easy row to hoe

but sure is kind & easy

next to this

"never again" feel like laughin in his face

THE NORTH STAR

knowin your way round the cotton field

is somethin' these women know

pickin & bundlin

draggin burlap sack filled with fresh cotton's

what they know

but now it's not the cotton on the ground

got their attention

this is a time to follow the north star

'cause that'll lead them to freedom somewhere 'way from here

they sang bout it / how the north star was goin to save them

they dreamed bout it huddled together in caves & under huge trees

& every night they were on their way north

closer to freedom

always followin the north star

TIME TUH GO

how can we let you go

we love you / we been doin all right here

it aint heaven but without you surely the devil

will be right at the door

you got to know what you plannin is dangerous

they kill runaways

sic dogs on them

or bring out the lash

you know that

but listen to me

ah jus' can't take it no more

ah am not some animal to be worked from dawn to dusk

livin on the entrails of hogs & such

ah am a livin bein' & ah got to be free

or ah am goin to kill somebody real soon

somebody white who don't even see me

ah don't want to be a killer

ah jus' want to be a free man

LOOK FOR THE BROKEN BRANCH

ah been walkin so far

don't exactly know where ah am or been

seen all kinds of folks

some of them don't even turn their heads when ah pass by

but they aint all friends that's for sure

but ah am lookin for one white man who's got a clue for me

to get to freedom wherever that is

how can ah know what white man to trust

if ah make a mistake only the good Lawd will know my fate

maybe ah do / though ah'll be one dead nigra

but ah got to look for this one good white man got a clue for me

wait / here comes one stoppin

reg'lar-lookin fella leanin over his horse

whisperin "look for the broken branch"

ah stand up & ah am on my way

ah come too far to turn back

STRANGER IN THE WOODS

who's that?

ah dunno / well he don't look like anybody ah know

we've gotta be careful he might be a spy for mastah

or tracker / or jus' be one of us / slippin on to freedom

best be quiet & still les' he notices us

whisper ah tell you / a stranger is a mighty dangerous

varmint / be one step ahead of the trackers

& them wicked dogs / dogs'll tear your

muscle right off the bone

right / can't be too careful

but he's travelin alone

can't we help him a little bit /

slap / now hush

DEATH OR FREEDOM

four colored folk & a beautiful colored chile

ready to march on to freedom

with the legend Sojourner Truth

one man hesitates

Sojourner Truth whips out a pistol

"death or freedom

either you comin wit' us

or us or you die heah

'cause we goin & you aint tellin nobody nothin bout us

you heah me?"

"ah aint goin to say a word Miz Truth, ah swear"

"don't matter, it's death or freedom"

the hammer of the gun clicks

it won't be the first time

THE SLAVE TRACKER

any African / slave or free

had call to turn they faces down

if treacherous john tanner

his helper & his hound

were bout

john tanner didn't care bout your manumission papers

or your papers showin you had bought your freedom

or your oath that you belonged to somebody awready

if you could look him in the eye / john tanner

he'd jus' as soon shoot you as sell you downriver

where blacks were used to whippins, nasty overseers

& watchin their infants pulled from they arms

& carried off by john tanner

was the reason

everbody of color turned they heads down

THE SACRIFICE

now

one of us gone didn't make it north

didn't make it to

freedom

them trackers caught his ankle in the swamp like a alligator

why didn't they jus' shoot him in the head

more they style

we comfort each other

weepin

contemplatin the torturous death of the other

a peculiar whimperin in the swamp

a peculiar grief on the way

to freedom

THE SWAMP

all kinds of critters movin in the swamp
tangles of roots wrapped round
& rolled over each other / me too
but ah got to be still / ah can't breathe full out
'cause then they might hear me
why ah got this here white shirt /
tryin to run to freedom /

dogs & trackers comin after me

my feet in water & weeds

my brow & my eyes drippin

with sweat so ah can't hardly see

best ah stay still / ah don't want to leave

no trail for the trackers

if they catch me / all they gonna

do is whip me till ah can't hardly stand

then drag me back to mastah

THE FINANCIER

he look jus' like mastah

oh but he aint

mastah have him killed

he have him killed / a abolitionist

give money to run the underground railroad

sure he got fine china & wineglasses

nice teacups & good manners

nevertheless

there's a price on his head

jus' like there's a price on our heads

he's jus' like us

trackers chasin him

bombs headin for his front room

a abolitionist a dangerous cause

dangerous state of mind

watch out / heah they come again

money or no

it's a idea will kill you

but our lives are as important as theirs

THE HOLE

ah hear 'em talkin / sashayin round

dancin they call it

make me laugh / but

that may mean the death of me

can't hardly breathe / if they hear me

Lawd make me quiet / so ah can live

my bones achin / my body freezin

Lawd quiet my soul / or

one of them slave hunters might forget

the party & come down here & capture me

me

ah become the party gift

or ah hush & get to canada

NEARLY THERE

the hosses are sweatin
we holdin our hats & the benches of the wagon
a-goin
a-goin
the trackers shootin at us
tryin to stop our way to freedom
the driver bringin that whip down
on the backs of them hosses
he shoutin "nearly there"
& we a-goin
a-goin
toward freedom
trackers tryin to kill us right this minute
"nearly there" the driver say
hoverin over so he can keep them hosses
live & runnin
runnin us to freedom
watch now
them trackers shootin at us again
stay low
stay low
"nearly there"

WELCOME TO MICHIGAN

been walkin

since mississippi got mo' clothes

& then snow on the ground

so cold

so cold

but freedom's nigh

these folks waitin in this weather

for us

they expectin us believin

we could make it to michigan

oh freedom's land

& we heah

we heah & these white folks

embracin us like we they own

they say "welcome to Michigan"

& we sure is happy to get heah

FREE AIR

finally ah am ridin through free air
ah got more folks with me
more folks' faces lookin toward freedom
we could sing & stomp our feet
get to feelin happy
plead with the Lawd we get to the border
fore trackers or some one white wanderer
let some sheriff know a kindly white soul
is riskin his life so we could have ours
Lawdy Lawdy we been blessed

Glory Hallelujah

I dedicate this, my third book on the Black American experience, to my grandson, Trevor Darian Harris, whom I will love a thousand lifetimes. —R.B.

When I was working on the paintings for this book, I was inspired by the field hollers, old Negro spirituals, and stories of southern folklore by Mark Twain. Images of slaves on plantations, sweating and working in the cotton fields from "can't see in the morning till can't see at night," called to me. I was haunted by their faces yearning for freedom, their bodies exhausted from their labors, and the harrowing escapes they made on the Underground Railroad. This book is my way of memorializing them and their struggles. —R.B.

Collins is an imprint of HarperCollins Publishers.
Amistad is an imprint of HarperCollins Publishers.

Freedom's a-Callin Me
Text copyright © 2012 by Ntozake Shange
Illustrations copyright © 2012 by Rod Brown

Library of Congress Cataloging-in-Publication Data
Shange, Ntozake.
Freedom's a-callin me / poems by Ntozake Shange ; paintings by Rod Brown. — 1st ed.
p. cm.
ISBN 978-0-06-133741-3 (trade bdg.)
ISBN 978-0-06-133743-7 (lib. bdg.)
I. Brown, Rod, date, ill. II. Title. III. Title: Freedom's a-calling me.
PS3569.H3324F65 2012   2010050515
[811'.54]—dc22   CIP
                                                                                          AC

Typography by Jennifer Rozbruch
12 13 14 15 16   SCP   10 9 8 7 6 5 4 3 2 1

❖
First Edition